To Ethan:

Thank you for your
awareness & support! I
hope you enjoy the book!

E. Mandel

This book is dedicated with all my love to Austin, the bravest and strongest boy I know. And to Levi and Nolan, the best, most supportive, and protective brothers. They each provide a constant source of joy and pride.

With special thanks to my loving husband Jon who continues to be the calm, optimistic voice throughout this journey.

www.mascotbooks.com

Austin's Allergies

For more information, please contact:
Mascot Books
620 Herndon Parkway, Suite 320
Herndon, VA 20170
info@mascotbooks.com

Library of Congress Control Number: 2018910177

CPSIA Code: PRT1118A
ISBN-13: 978-1-64307-147-3

Printed in the United States

AUSTIN'S ALLERGIES

Erin Mandras   Illustrated by Nina Kolbe

Hi! You can call me Austin.
Let me tell you about myself.
Come on in!

I'm four years old
and love to race my
toy cars.
But what I like most
is swinging from the
monkey bars.

My skin was red, dry, and itchy,
and my tummy was sore.
So my mommy and daddy took me
to the doctor to find out more.

Going to the doctor can make me
really scared,
But my mommy said I shouldn't
worry, because the doctor only
cared.

The doctor gently held my arm and told me it would just be a prick. When it was all done, I said, "That was quick!"

The doctor said there are foods I'm allergic to,
But they can't stop me from what I love to do.

Wheat, eggs, milk, peanuts, and tree nuts I stay away from.
They're not safe to eat, not even a crumb.

If I eat something I'm allergic to, I will feel sick. I can throw up or have trouble breathing, so someone needs to come quick.

I'm too little to carry my own medicine kit,
So a grown-up who is with me must always have it.

Epinephrine is the medicine that goes in my thigh,
The shot makes me feel better after ten seconds go by.

I was so brave when
I needed a shot of
epinephrine,
And now I know I'll be
okay if I need it again.

There are two things I do to stay healthy and happy:

I wash my hands when I eat, and I only eat food from my mommy and daddy.

Washing hands with soap and water is my number one rule. It helps keep me safe, especially in school.

I wear a bracelet with my name on it, and my friends think it's cool. It lists my food allergies as a safety tool.

They say I'm the best at sharing my toys and games.
I always play nicely with my cool planes and trains.

But when it comes to food, if
I'm offered a snack,
I remember to be safe, and
must stand back.

Birthday parties are so much fun!
I'm always on the run.

But when it's time for
pizza and cake and we
take our seats,
I grab my box filled with
my favorite treats.

Fruit snacks, lollipops,
and safe cookies, too,
Are three of my treats
I usually stick to.

My mommy and daddy tell everyone they know. They want me to be safe, healthy, and able to grow.

Food allergies
are just a small
part of me.
But I do love to
hear something
is allergy-free.

My mommy and daddy read every label
To make sure only safe food is put on the table.

I may have to
eat food that is
allergy-free,
But there is so
much more you
can say about me.

We can color, play catch, build with blocks, or make up something fun!
But when I'm around, please make sure safety is number one!

About the Author

Erin Mandras is a mother to three boys: Levi, Austin, and Nolan. She and her husband Jon, a dentist, reside in Baltimore, Maryland. Erin's passion for helping others has led her down a path of writing and speaking. Her son, Austin, has multiple life-threatening food allergies, and as a result of her personal experiences, she is on a mission to raise awareness and educate others.

Erin also publicly speaks and writes for *Kick the Scale* on eating disorders, body image, and exercise all based around her story of developing, battling, and overcoming an eating disorder as a college athlete. Her story and more information can be found at kickthescale.com.

About the Illustrator

Nina Kolbe lives in Troy, Michigan, where she works as a general and trauma surgeon. She is also a mother of three: Alessandra, Cecilia, and Lucas. Her husband, Nick, is a 5th grade teacher for Troy School District. As a mother and a physician, Nina thinks the work Erin is doing to raise awareness of food allergies is incredibly important. She is thrilled to be a part of this book and hopes it has an impact on educating others about this vital issue.

Nina and Erin are the best of friends. They played soccer together at Michigan State University and were roommates all four years of college. Their families remain close, making this publication that much more special.

Austin says: My favorite treat is chocolate cake from The Really Great Food Company! It's free from the top 8 allergen foods and super delicious! It's also kosher and GMO free! You can pick some up from my website, austinsallergies.com.